5S

WASHOE COUNTY LIBRARY

3 1235 03274 5379

W9-CQZ-806

2 8 2007

WATERMELON WISHES

by Lisa Moser

Illustrated by
Stacey Schuett

Clarion Books ● New York

Clarion Books
a Houghton Mifflin Company imprint
215 Park Avenue South, New York, NY 10003

Text copyright © 2006 by Lisa Moser
Illustrations copyright © 2006 by Stacey Schuett

The illustrations were executed in acrylic and gouache on Arches paper.
The text was set in 15-point ITC Bookman.

All rights reserved.

For information about permission to reproduce selections from this book, write to
Permissions, Houghton Mifflin Company, 215 Park Avenue South, New York, NY 10003.

www.houghtonmifflinbooks.com

Printed in China

Library of Congress Cataloging-in-Publication Data

Moser, Lisa. Watermelon wishes / by Lisa Moser ; illustrated by Stacey Schuett.
p. cm. Summary: When Charlie spends the summer growing watermelons with
his grandfather, his secret wish is to do it all over again the next year.
ISBN 0-618-56433-0
[1. Watermelons—Fiction. 2. Grandfathers—Fiction. 3. Wishes—Fiction.]
I. Schuett, Stacey, ill. II. Title.
PZ7.M84696Wa 2006   [E]—dc22   2005000656

ISBN-13: 978-0-618-56433-0   ISBN-10: 0-618-56433-0

SCP 10 9 8 7 6 5 4 3 2 1

For Mom and Dad,
with love and gratitude
—L. M.

For Grandpa Butch
—S. S.

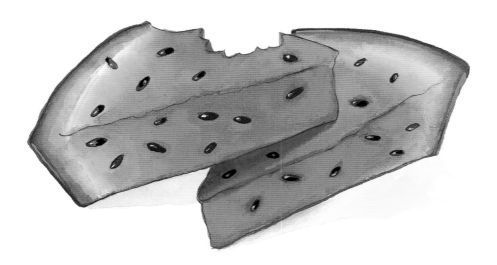

S till got 'em?" asked Grandpap.

"Yes," said Charlie. He patted his pocket to make double sure.

"That's my boy." Grandpap opened the shed door.

Charlie found a spade and a trowel. Grandpap grabbed the watering can. They piled everything into the wheelbarrow with the squeaky wheel.

Squeak! Squeak! Squeak!

"Still got 'em?" asked Grandpap.

"Yep," said Charlie.

Grandpap drove the spade into the sandy soil.

Charlie crawled around on his knees, pushing the dirt into big hills.

"Still got 'em?" asked Grandpap.

"Right here," said Charlie. He pulled the seeds from his pocket.

"You plant the seeds," said Grandpap. "I'll fill the watering can."

Tired, Charlie leaned against Grandpap. "We'll grow great watermelons," said Charlie.

Grandpap wiped his face with a red bandanna. "Think so?"

"Maybe even a wishing watermelon," said Charlie.

"What's a wishing watermelon?" asked Grandpap.

"You'll see," Charlie told him.

Charlie and Grandpap woke up early every morning
and worked in their garden. Grandpap hoed a prickly
thistle. "Tell me more about this wishing watermelon."

Charlie pulled a sneaky weed. "It's a very special
watermelon. And it can give only one wish."

"There are a lot of things a fella might want," said
Grandpap. "Do you have a wish?"

Charlie nodded.

"Bet I can guess it," said Grandpap.

"You can try," said Charlie.

"When I was a boy, I wanted a dog," said Grandpap. "You're going to wish for a dog." Charlie shook his head.

When the first green shoots poked up, Charlie and Grandpap picnicked by the garden. Grandpap unpacked the sandwiches and cookies. Charlie poured lemonade from the thermos into the cup they shared. They took turns spotting new sprouts.

Afterwards, they strolled the dirt path home. Grandpap unwrapped a butterscotch and handed it to Charlie. "I know what you'll wish for," said Grandpap. "Butterscotch. A whole bushel basket of butterscotch."

Charlie grinned. "No. That's not it."

When yellow flowers bloomed on the vines, Charlie and Grandpap celebrated. They rode their bikes to Grandpap's secret fishing spot. Charlie dug up worms. Grandpap tied a hook and line to branches he found along the shore. Then they sat on the grassy bank and watched their bobbers.

"Maybe you'll wish for a fishing pole," said Grandpap.
"A slick new rod with a shiny reel."
"I don't think so," said Charlie.

When evening shadows crept across the garden, Charlie and Grandpap played basketball. Charlie climbed the hay bales and pulled the peach basket to the top. "Okay, shoot."

Grandpap dribbled the basketball. *Thunk, thunk, thunk.* He heaved the ball in the air. *Rattle, rattle, thud!*

Charlie cheered and fished the ball out of the basket. "My turn!" he yelled, jumping down.

Grandpap raised the basket. "Hey, maybe you should wish for a real basketball hoop," said Grandpap. "That'd be a good wish."

Charlie just laughed. *Rattle, rattle, thud!*

One hot day, Charlie and Grandpap counted ten small watermelons growing on the vines. Then they piled into the old truck, and Grandpap drove to the swimming hole.

Charlie swam and splashed. Grandpap bobbed along in an inner tube.

"Now I know for certain," said Grandpap. "You're gonna wish for your very own swimming pool."

"Nope," said Charlie, floating by.

Even when the watermelons grew fatter and greener, Grandpap was still guessing.

"A red scooter? A new baseball glove? A giant ham sandwich?"

"No, no, no." Charlie laughed. "You won't guess."

"Maybe you're right," said Grandpap.

One morning in August, Charlie looked out the kitchen window. "Today we'll find the wishing watermelon," he announced.

Grandpap jumped to his feet. "Yahoo! Let's go!"

Charlie looked over the watermelon patch, and
Grandpap pointed to different watermelons.

"How about that one?"
"Too big."
"That one?"
"Too small."
"There are three good ones over there," said Grandpap.
"Too lumpy, too dirty, too squishy," said Charlie.

Charlie walked to the edge of the garden. He peeked
under a pile of leaves. "Perfect! Here's the wishing
watermelon."

Grandpap lifted the watermelon into the wheelbarrow.
Together they pushed the wishing watermelon to the
house.

Squeak! Squeak! Squeak!

"I'm ready to make my wish," said Charlie.

"Great!" said Grandpap.

Charlie closed his eyes for only a moment. "Quick! My wish will be inside the watermelon."

Grandpap cut a hole in the watermelon.

Charlie stuck his hand inside. *Squish! Spluck! Slurp!* His fingers curled around the secret. "My wish came true!" he shouted.

Grandpap clapped his hands. "What was the wish?"

Charlie opened his hand and showed Grandpap
the small black watermelon seeds.
"I wished for another summer just like this one."

31

Grandpap took the seeds from Charlie's hands and wiped them clean. Carefully, he slid them into Charlie's front pocket. He tapped the pocket over Charlie's heart.

"Got 'em?" asked Grandpap.

"Always," said Charlie. He leaned his head on Grandpap's shoulder and took a juicy bite of watermelon.